JILL AND THE BIG CAT

Text by Etho Rothstein
Illustrations by Maureen Paxton

Black Moss Press

Jill is a beautiful dog
and she knows it!
Her coat of black silky hair has a bit of a wave in it.
Her feet and chest are white and the end of her tail
has just a fleck of white.

Her eyes make people think of chocolate.
There is hardly anyone who doesn't like chocolate.

Jill lives on Capilano Road.
Here the mountains reach to the sky
and the forests hug the slopes.
Jill has never explored the forest.

She is happy in her back yard.
She has her own bed near the back door and
a red dish for her dinner.

She has her own raincoat for the rainy weather.
It rains most of the time.

Jill takes care of the yard.
She chases other dogs and cats away and
sometimes she even snarls—Grrr!

Jill tries to be the best dog of all.
When other dogs bark, Jill barks louder.
When other dogs run after cars, Jill runs faster.

But when the other dogs run after cats, Jill just watches.
She knows that cats can climb trees and slip
through fences and do many things that dogs can't do.

Cats are all right in their place,
but not in Jill's yard.

One day, a strange cat walked through Jill's gate.
The cat's nose and tail were held high in the air.

It was a very imperious cat.
Jill was furious!
She bounded towards the cat, snarling and growling—Grrr.

The cat stood on tiptoes.
Its legs were stiff.
Its fur and tail stood straight up.
It arched its back.
It looked HUGE.

Then it spit at Jill.
Jill was so frightened that she ran away.

What a puzzle it was, that a small cat could suddenly
become so big.
It would be a good trick for *her* to use
if she ever had the chance.

The next morning when she awoke, dogs were barking.
What was all the fuss?

When Jill went up the road,
she couldn't believe her eyes!
There was the biggest cat she had ever seen.
Jill was frightened—until she remembered
the cat trick.

Jill stood on tiptoes.
Her legs were stiff.
Her fur and tail stood up.
Her back was arched.
She looked H U G E.

When the cat saw such a large fierce dog
it jumped up into a tree.
It stayed there until some men came.

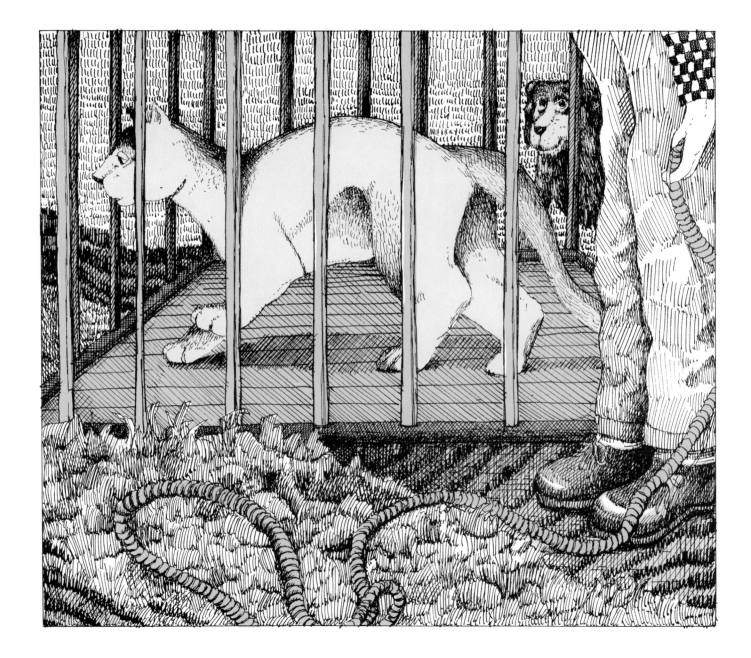

They threw a rope around its neck and pulled
it to the ground.
Then the cat was put into a cage.

People gathered around and praised Jill
for being such a brave dog.
"Just imagine," the people said.
"Jill has frightened a cougar!"

Jill was proud.
But she wondered—hmm.
Cougar?
She did not know a cat named Cougar on Capilano.
But one thing she did know.
Cougar would never come near her yard again.

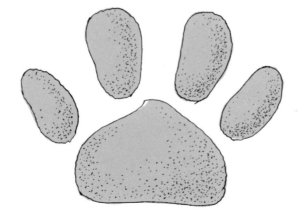

Second printing

Published by Black Moss Press, P.O. Box 143, Station A, Windsor, Ontario. Distributed in Canada and the U.S. by Firefly Books. All orders should be directed to 3520 Pharmacy Ave., Unit 1-C, Scarborough, Ontario, Canada.

Acknowledgement for financial assistance towards publication of this book is due to the Canada Council and the Ontario Arts Council.

First printing September 1984

ISBN 0-88753-112-1

Printed in Canada